Contents

Chapter One	7
Chapter Two	21
Chapter Three	35
Chapter Four	47
Chapter Five	65
Chapter Six	85
Chapter Seven	97
Chapter Eight	111

Chapter One

Poppy Merrymoss's wings fluttered excitedly as she gazed up at the giant old oak tree. She had dreamed about going to Oakwings Academy her whole life and now it was finally happening!

All around her, hundreds of excited fairies hustled and bustled about as they flew in and out of the school.

Poppy had never seen so many fairies
in one place before, or so many
beautiful wings and outfits. Some wore
hats made from acorn cups or flowers.
Others had tops and trousers made
from colourful petals. There was even
a fairy dressed from
head to toe in
feathers. Poppy
felt dizzy
looking at
them all.

   "Did you
know Oakwings
has its own

swimming pond?" a young fairy said as she flitted past.

"I heard there is a stargazing room!" said another.

Poppy spotted a snow fairy and gasped. The fairy had long white hair and crystal wings which sparkled in the sunlight. Snow fairies were really rare. Poppy fluttered up and down, full of nerves and excitement as she wondered for the millionth time which type of fairy she might become. She wouldn't find out until she had learned how to use her fairy magic. She looked up at the enormous tree again and gulped.

Oakwings Academy was bigger than any tree she had ever seen. She was used to being small – she was a fairy after all – but she suddenly felt tiny. How was she ever going to find her way around? What if she was no good at magic?

Poppy's mum squeezed her hand. "Aunt Lily will be here soon to show you around," she said.

"Did someone say my name?" A sing-songy voice trilled from above.

Poppy could always spot Aunt Lily a mile away. She had blazing red hair and wore the most beautiful flower petal dresses. Nut shell bracelets jingled and jangled around her wrists, and a fluffy white dandelion seed hung from each of her ears. Above one ear was the cochlear implant which helped her hear better.

Poppy hugged her aunt as she landed beside her. "Hi, Aunt Lily."

She smelled like roses and sunshine, and Poppy felt less nervous. Aunt Lily was a petal fairy and a teacher at Oakwings Academy. Poppy was glad that she knew at least one fairy at her new school.

Aunt Lily beamed, then tried to look

serious. "Remember to call me Ms Mayblossom while you're at school, Poppy," she said, trying to sound stern.

Poppy giggled. "Sorry, Aunt . . . Ms Mayblossom."

Aunt Lily glanced around, then whispered, "Of course, I suppose we could break the rules just once!"

She pulled Poppy into another big, squishy hug. "Let's get you settled in, shall we?"

"We'll see you very soon," Poppy's dad said.

"You'll have a wonderful time," her mum added in a wobbly voice.

Poppy gave them each a long hug, then bent down to say goodbye to her baby sister, Daisy, who planted a dribbly kiss on her cheek.

Poppy wiped her face, took a deep breath and followed Aunt Lily . . . *Ms Mayblossom,* she reminded herself, into the old oak tree.

It was even busier inside. They flew into a great hall filled with fairy teachers and students, old and new. Poppy weaved in and out of the crowd. Aunt Lily waved and greeted fairies as she flew. Everyone seemed to know her. A few fairies gazed curiously at Poppy

and she smiled back at them.

Aunt Lily led Poppy down a corridor. Poppy peered into the classrooms as they passed. In one room, a fairy waved his wand as large droplets of water danced around him in the air. Another was filled with shelves of small glass jars containing a rainbow of colourful liquids. *I can't wait until I can do magic like that!* Poppy thought excitedly.

They continued up and around a winding staircase, until they reached the highest branches.

"These are the bedrooms," Aunt Lily explained. She landed outside a wide, wooden door and pushed it open.

Poppy barely had the chance to step inside when a blur of pink wings rushed towards her.

"Hi, roomie!" the fairy called out.

Her hair was in long black braids which trailed behind her as she flew, and she wore a bright pink petal dress. She whizzed around the room, her wings buzzing.

Poppy glanced around. The room had curved walls and two bunk beds, one on either side of a small round window. At one of the beds, another fairy was unpacking a pile of fancy-looking conker shell suitcases.

"Hello! I'm Rose Seedpip," the flying fairy said breathlessly. She pointed at the other fairy. "That's Celeste Greenshoot. I'm so excited to be here, aren't you? Everything is so magical,

and HUGE and I can't wait to start lessons. What type of fairy do you want to be?" she asked in a big rush of words.

Poppy laughed. Rose talked as fast as she flew and Poppy already liked her.

"Will you stay still!" Celeste snapped at Rose. "You're making me dizzy."

Celeste had curly blonde hair and silver wings. Her top and skirt were made from purple pansies and her shoes had curled toes and a tiny bell on each end.

"They were hand-crafted by mice especially for me," Celeste said, seeing Poppy staring at them.

"They're beautiful," Poppy said, with a smile. "I'm Poppy Merrymoss."

But Celeste had turned back to her unpacking.

"Nice to meet you, Poppy," Rose replied as she landed with a bit of a bump.

She pointed to the top of the other bunk bed. "That's my bunk," she said. "The bottom one is yours. Watch!"

The wooden headboard of Poppy's bed began to glow. Slowly, golden letters appeared, magically carving her name into the wood.

Poppy grinned as she traced her

name with her finger. She still couldn't believe she was finally here!

"Isn't it amazing!" Rose breathed.

Poppy couldn't help but agree. Everything at Oakwings Academy was so wonderful.

A gentle cough came from the doorway and Poppy jumped. She'd been so caught up in the excitement that she'd forgotten Aunt Lily was still there!

"I'll leave you to make friends, Poppy" she whispered with a smile. "Welcome to fairy forest school."

Chapter Two

As soon as Aunt Lily had left, there
was a flash of purple smoke, and
Poppy's battered chestnut shell suitcases
magically appeared in the room.
Celeste continued to ignore Poppy and
Rose as she pulled what seemed like
endless pairs of shoes out of her own
suitcases. Poppy and Rose chatted
away happily as they unpacked.

"Where I live it's freezing and it snows all the time," Rose said.

"I've never even seen snow!" Poppy exclaimed. Just then a bluebell hanging on the wall jingled back and forth suddenly, surprising them both.

"What was that?" Rose squealed, stumbling backwards.

Celeste rolled her eyes. "It's just the bell," she said. "It means it's time to go to assembly."

"How do you know that?" Poppy asked.

Celeste flicked her curly hair over her shoulder. "My big sister Serena already

22

goes here," she explained. "In fact, she's the Head Girl this year, just like *I* will be one day."

Rose poked her tongue out at Celeste as she flew out of the bedroom, and Poppy giggled. She linked arms with Rose and they followed after Celeste, flying down and around the spiral staircase to the great hall in the very roots of the old oak tree. The fairies didn't really need the stairs, but they were there for any animal visitors.

It was already crowded when they arrived and they were jostled around by some bigger fairies as they continued to file in.

"Hey! Watch it!" Poppy shouted.

Rose pulled her over to one side so they wouldn't get knocked over.

"Where do we sit?" she asked.

The room was huge and grand. Poppy felt very tiny again as she gazed around at the walls. Images of all the different types of fairies and magic they used were carved into the wood. Water, wind, sunshine, tree, animal, snow and many more. At the front of the hall a large round window let in bright sunlight which warmed the air. Tiny crystals floated magically above, and when the sun hit them, the room sparkled.

Celeste was with the other new students sitting at the front of the hall. Poppy and Rose flew over to join her.

As they waited nervously for their head teacher, Madame Brightglow, to arrive, the fairy beside Poppy jolted her with his elbow.

"Ow!" Poppy said, turning with a glare.

But her scowl soon turned into a smile as she recognised him. "Ninad!" she cried.

"This is Ninad Clearwater, we went to Fairy Nursery together," Poppy explained to Rose. "I'm so happy you're here," she told Ninad, glad to see another friendly face at Oakwings.

Ninad brushed his messy dark brown

hair out of his eyes and pushed his glasses up his nose, giving Rose and Celeste a shy smile.

"What's that?" Rose asked, peering at something behind Ninad.

"This is Spot," Ninad said proudly. "He's my pet ladybird."

Spot lifted up one of his front legs in a wave. Poppy and Rose waved back.

The ladybird climbed onto Ninad's lap and plonked himself down.

"Oof! He's heavier than he looks," Ninad said, stroking Spot's head.

"Do you think we're going to get our wands?" Poppy wondered as the voices in the hall grew louder.

"I hope so!" Rose replied. "I can't wait to finally have my very own wand! Did you know that the type of wand you get can give you a clue about what type of fairy you will be?" she gabbled. "Both of my mums are snow fairies," she continued, "but that doesn't mean that I will be one."

"Wow!" Ninad said, awestruck. "I've never seen a snow fairy before."

Rose glanced at Celeste. "They are *very* rare," she boasted loudly. "Although," she said, lowering her voice, "they're not as rare where I live in the Snowflake Mountains!"

"My dad wants me to be a water fairy like him," Ninad moaned, "but I'm much more interested in animal magic."

"I'm not sure what type of fairy I want to be," Poppy admitted. "My dad is a tree fairy and Mum is a wind fairy. I want to learn all kinds of magic."

I just hope I'm not terrible at it, she thought to herself.

"I already know what I'm going to be," Celeste interrupted. "A sunshine fairy."

The others gasped.

"Madame Brightglow is a sunshine fairy," Ninad said, his eyes wide. "They are *very* rare."

"And powerful," Rose added.

Celeste gave them a smug look. "*And* their wands are made from ash trees. The wood helps with the heat of the sunshine magic. That's the kind of wand *I'll* be getting," she said, looking very sure of herself.

"I'd love to see the look on her

face if she got no wand at all!" Rose whispered.

Ninad snickered, but Poppy felt an icy chill rush through her. "Could that happen?" she asked. What if she didn't receive a wand at all? Would she have to leave Oakwings Academy?

"I meant Celeste could be a fungus fairy," Rose explained. "They don't use wands to do magic. They like using toadstools and mushrooms instead."

Poppy hoped she wouldn't be one of those. It wasn't that she didn't want to be a fungus fairy, but she had dreamed of the moment she got her wand. It was all part of the magic of being a fairy.

A sudden quiet filled the room as
Madame Brightglow
flew to the front.
Her wings
were golden,
shining in
the sunlight.
Her dress was
made of yellow
daffodils and
she wore a yellow
primrose-flower hat on her head.
Everything about her seemed to glow
with sunshiny warmth.

"That's a *real* sunshine fairy," Rose whispered to Celeste, and Celeste narrowed her eyes in return.

Madame Brightglow cast her twinkling eyes over the fairies. "I'm delighted to welcome our new fairies to Oakwings Academy," she said, her voice loud and clear. "You will shortly be receiving your wands," she continued. There was a buzz of excitement around the room, and Madame Brightglow smiled. "They will not only help you do magic on your own, but they will give you a hint about what type of fairy you might become. Some types of wood work better with certain types of magic. Water fairies, for example, usually have wands made of willow. Sunshine fairies have wands made from ash." She held her wand in the air for all to see.

Poppy's heart raced so fast she thought she could almost hear it beating. Madame Brightglow caught her eye and gave Poppy a kind smile.

"First years, hold out your hands," she ordered. "You are about to receive your fairy wands."

Chapter Three

Warm sunshine filled the room. Poppy's skin tingled with excitement, and Rose could barely sit still beside her. Something wonderful was about to happen!

In the blink of an eye, something appeared in her grasp. *Her wand!* Her wings fluttered excitedly but she was too nervous to look at the wand in her hand. Instead, she glanced over at her friends. Ninad held a willow wand. He sighed and waved it back and forth like it was just an old stick, not something that could create magic. Poppy shot him a sympathetic glance.

Celeste was delighted with her wand. She held it in the air so that everyone could see. It was made from ash, which meant she was probably going to be a rare sunshine fairy just as she'd said.

"What did you get?" Poppy whispered to Rose.

Rose held up her wand, her eyebrows raised. "It's eucalyptus," she said. "They

are usually used by wind fairies."

She nudged Poppy's arm. "Are you happy with your wand?"

"I can't look!" Poppy said.

Rose frowned. "Why not?"

"I'm worried it might not be very good," Poppy admitted.

Rose laughed. "*All* wands are good, Poppy. They help us do magic!"

Poppy slowly held out her wand and peeked down at it. It was made from oak. Long and smooth and slightly crooked. "It's perfect!" she cried.

Oak wands were the only type which worked with all kinds of fairy magic.

Poppy felt strangely relieved that she
still had no idea which type of fairy
she might be. She wanted to learn spells
and magic of all kinds!

A spark of bright light shot into the
air. Madame Brightglow lowered her
wand and the room fell silent.

"Wands are one of the most important things a fairy needs to do their job," Madame Brightglow began. "Our mission is to help nature. When we use our magic for good, the forest rewards us with a magical seed. These seeds grow into plants filled with magical fairy dust so we can help the forest and the whole fairy kingdom. Without the seeds, we have no magic, and without magic the forest will die."

Poppy's mouth fell open. She knew how important fairy magic was, but she hadn't realised that the forest could die without it!

"You will learn to use magic to help the animals in the forest," Madame Brightglow told them. "How to plant the seeds and look after the flowers and trees, the rivers and streams. Even the weather. When you have learned everything you need to know from your wonderful teachers, you will discover what type of fairy you are."

Celeste sat up straight. "I *already* know I'm going to be a sunshine fairy," she whispered. "My wand proves it."

Madame Brightglow shot a warning glare at Celeste. "Your type of wand does not determine what type of fairy

you will be; it just gives you a clue. The rest is up to you!"

More fairies joined Madame Brightglow at the front of the hall. Poppy spotted Aunt Lily and gave her a small wave. Aunt Lily winked back.

"These are your teachers," Madame Brightglow said. "Each of them are experts in their area of fairy magic."

She smiled at the fairy beside her. "And I'm delighted to introduce our new deputy head, Ms Webcap."

Poppy stared at Ms Webcap. She wore a small, round black hat on her head, and her long blonde hair glistened with dewdrop-covered spiderwebs. Her skirt was a round mushroom, and she wore a short cape made from brown leaves.

"She's a fungus fairy," Rose whispered dramatically. "The most mysterious fairy type."

Poppy couldn't help staring – she'd never seen a fungus fairy before. As she looked, two beady black eyes seemed to peer back at her from Ms Webcap's hat. Poppy blinked in surprise but they had disappeared. Poppy shook her head. She must be imagining things!

"I am so pleased to be teaching here at Oakwings Academy," Ms Webcap said. "And seeing what all of you can do."

Madame Brightglow turned back to the new fairies. "Before lessons begin —" She paused as the room grew dark. A murmur of voices rose as everyone wondered what was going on. Poppy looked to the teachers but they seemed just as confused as she was.

Then a wicked cackle filled the air.

Rose grabbed hold of Poppy's arm and Ninad trembled beside her. They stared as a shadowy figure hovered in the middle of the hall. Glittering silver letters appeared in the air:

Each and every type of fairy –
Fire, water, snow – be wary . . .
Through my curse and wicked deeds,
No longer will you get your magic seeds.

At the bottom, swirly words shone:
Lady Nightshade.

As suddenly as they had appeared,

the words and dark figure disappeared and sunlight returned.

A rush of ice flooded through Poppy. Ninad looked as though he had seen a ghost, and Rose looked like she was about to be sick.

"Lady Nightshade?" Poppy gasped. "Isn't she just a story?"

All young fairies knew the tales about Lady Nightshade, an evil fairy who wanted to destroy the forest.

Celeste rolled her eyes. "Everyone knows Lady Nightshade is just a myth to scare little fairies into washing their wings. But she isn't *real.*"

Poppy thought Celeste didn't look as sure as she sounded.

"She seemed pretty real to me," Rose muttered.

"What does it mean?" Poppy wondered. "If fairies can't get magic seeds any more, what will happen to the forest and everyone who lives here?"

She looked to her friends, but none of them seemed to have the answer. Even Celeste stayed quiet. Poppy knew one thing though — whoever Lady Nightshade was, she clearly meant trouble!

Chapter Four

The bluebell rang loudly, shocking everyone into silence.

"The teachers and I have everything in hand," Madame Brightglow said, after a moment. "Someone is playing a prank and, believe me, I'll find out who. I don't want anyone to worry about this so-called Lady Nightshade. Concentrate on your lessons and becoming the best fairies you can be."

With that, the fairy teachers flew into action. They began shouting out orders and gathering their classes, leading them out of the hall, until Poppy's class were the only ones left.

One of the teachers waved his hand at them, trying to get their attention. He had grey hair which stuck up at all angles, and wore a brightly patterned waistcoat and patchwork trousers. He pushed a pair of wire-rimmed glasses up his nose. "First years!" he shouted above the noise, finally getting their attention. "Follow me."

Poppy stayed close to Rose and Ninad as they followed the teacher. Celeste flew to the front of the line to be next to the teacher.

"My name is Mr Pitterpour," the teacher said, in a quiet but firm voice. "I am a water fairy and will be teaching your first lesson. Follow me!"

"But what about Lady Nightshade?" Poppy asked. "Aren't we going to do something?"

A few of the other students nodded at her question.

Mr Pitterpour frowned at the floor as he seemed to search for an answer.

"The best thing we can do is continue our lessons and take care of the forest," he said.

He turned and flew along the hallway. The class followed behind, chatting excitedly, but Poppy still felt there must be something more they could be doing.

They reached a classroom and fluttered inside. The room was circular, with smooth tree bark walls. Desks were arranged in a circle around a long wooden table in the centre of the room, covered in ancient-looking maps showing far-away places that Poppy had never even heard of.

"This is the map room," Mr
Pitterpour said, smiling at them. "It
is where many adventures begin.
Including yours."

He stood at the table, and Poppy and
the others gathered around. Celeste
elbowed her way between two fairies
to get the best view.

"This," Mr Pitterpour said, waving his willow wand from one end of the table to the other, "is a map of Fairy Kingdom."

Poppy moved forward for a closer look. Fairy Kingdom was bigger than she had ever imagined. She scanned the map, looking at the different place names. There was a colourful patch of butterflies called Butterfly Meadow. Some snow covered mountains called the Snowflake Mountains, which Rose pointed out in delight. Poppy was searching for her home when she was interrupted by Mr Pitterpour.

He flicked the end of his wand and a small orange spark appeared. It floated down, landing on the map, and glowed brightly.

"That is Raindrop River," Mr Pitterpour told them, pointing at a long, wavy blue line that weaved through the entire forest. "And it is where we will be going today."

Rose grabbed Poppy's arm and flapped up and down, squealing in delight. "We're going to learn some magic!"

Despite her worry about Lady Nightshade, Poppy laughed and

jumped with her. Even Ninad, who had been sulking about getting a willow wand, perked up.

Mr Pitterpour tapped his wand on the map and commanded, "RAINDROP RIVER!" Suddenly the air around them shimmered. Tiny lights slowly circled the fairies, spinning faster and faster until everything was a blur. Just as Poppy was starting to feel giddy and a little bit sick, the lights faded.

Poppy blinked. They were no longer in the map room. They were surrounded by lush green leaves and the tinkling sound of water from a

nearby waterfall. They were in the forest, right beside Raindrop River.

Poppy gaped at the waterfall in wonder. Each tiny water drop shone with a rainbow.

"Watch closely," Mr Pitterpour told them. "We are going to learn the raindrop spell. It works with any type of water."

He held out his wand to catch a droplet of water. The wand absorbed the drop, then another and another as though it was drinking it up.

"Just concentrate on catching the water drop and your fairy wand will do the rest," he said.

The fairies gathered along the river. Ninad went first and managed to collect a few drops right away.

"Excellent, Ninad," Mr Pitterpour nodded approvingly.

Ninad frowned but continued collecting water.

Poppy held out her wand. The water was flowing so quickly it was difficult to catch a single drop. She focused on the little rainbows

instead, and imagined her wand sucking up the water like a straw. She felt time slow as she concentrated. A single drop fell in slow motion and she held her wand to it. The tip sparked with a tiny blue light as she caught the drop. "I did it!" she cried.

Rose, however, was not doing as well. "The water keeps moving *away* from me," she huffed.

Poppy watched Rose. Rose held her wand out, her face twisted in concentration. But instead of catching a drop, the water spurted out in all directions like a fountain.

Celeste screamed as she got soaked.

Rose blushed. "It was an accident," she cried. "Sorry, Celeste."

Celeste narrowed her eyes at Rose as she squeezed water out of her hair. "She soaked me on purpose, Mr Pitterpour!"

"It's only water, Celeste," Mr Pitterpour said, trying to hide his smile. "I'll help you dry off."

He twirled the end of his wand. A gust of wind spun around Celeste, starting at her feet and twisting all the way up to the top of her head.

Celeste looked down at herself in wonder. "I'm dry!" she gasped. Everyone giggled.

Poppy couldn't help laughing.

"What are you lot all looking at?" Celeste snapped. Then she caught her reflection in the river. Her hair was stood up on end as though she'd

been caught in a hurricane! Celeste
screamed in horror.

"At least you're dry," Mr Pitterpour
said. He turned to the rest of the class.
"Let's try something else. Try to collect
raindrops from the leaves and then take
the water to the animals who need it."

Small animals had gathered along
the riverbank, watching the fairies
at work. Tiny doors and holes were
dotted along the riverbank and in the
tree trunks. There were small rabbits,
moles, dormice and small birds in the
branches above.

Poppy collected water from a leaf

and poured it into a large conker shell. An otter padded over and held out her paws. Poppy smiled and handed her the shell.

"Thank you," said the otter. "That was brilliant!"

"Really?" Poppy asked, pleased.

"I'm Ottalie," the otter said. "Me and my family live right over there." She pointed to a little house on the riverbank, with lots of baby otters playing outside it.

Poppy hugged the little otter. "I'm Poppy. Nice to meet you."

All along the river, fairies delivered

water to animals in need. A bunny and her babies hopped and bounced around them as fairies filled small wooden buckets and shells.

Poppy headed to the river for more water and found Rose and Ninad

doing the same.

"Look!" Ninad smiled, pointing to the family of otters, who were now playing in the river.

Ottalie was swimming on her back as a tiny otter splashed her with water.

That's Ottalie," Poppy said, waving.

Ottalie swam over to them. "This is my baby brother Ollie."

"He's so cute!" Rose said.

Ninad flew over and Ollie gave him a hug. Ninad giggled as Ollie tried to nibble his hair.

"Ollie, that's not food!" Ottalie called.

Ninad laughed and led him back to Ottalie.

Despite worrying about Lady Nightingale, Poppy felt a warm glow inside as she helped the animals. Fairy magic was even better than she had ever imagined!

Chapter Five

"Good morning, sleepywings!"

Poppy groaned and opened one eye to see Rose grinning at her she hung upside down from her bunk above.

"We're late for breakfast," Rose said. "It's maple pancakes day today. My favourite!"

She swung from the bed and flipped in the air, flying a little too fast.

"Slow down!" Poppy warned, but it was too late. Rose bumped into the wall, then the bed, then fell backwards to the floor with a *THUMP*!

"Are you OK?" Poppy laughed.

Rose rubbed her bottom and grinned back.

Celeste huffed loudly from her side of the room as she tried to pick a dress from the pile on her bed.

"There's not enough space in here!" She glared at Poppy and Rose as though it were their fault.

Rose put her hand on her hip. "You have *two* beds, Celeste," she said. "Twice

the space that me and Poppy have. You don't hear us moaning, do you?"

Celeste snorted. "That's because you don't have as many clothes and shoes as I do. My bedroom at home is as big as the great hall," she boasted. "And my closet is twice as big as this room."

Rose opened her mouth to reply but Poppy quickly pulled her out of the room before her friend could say anything she'd regret.

"She only needs more space so that she can fit in that big head of hers," Rose grumbled as they flew down to have their breakfast.

Poppy could smell the food before they entered the great hall. Wonderful wafts of maple pancakes, blueberries and plum porridge filled the air. Rows of wooden tables filled the hall, each laden with delicious food. Poppy spotted Ninad and waved as she and Rose sat down to join him.

"*Mmff mfm mm mfmf*," Ninad said, his mouth full. His ladybird Spot crawled along the table, stealing crumbs.

"What?" Poppy asked.

Ninad swallowed his food. "I said, you have got to try these." He lifted a plate piled high with sticky, gooey, honey-covered buns.

Rose grabbed one and shoved it into her mouth in one go. She sighed in delight as she ate and gave Ninad a thumbs up.

Just like everything else at Oakwings Academy, the food was magical.

No matter how many buns Ninad
ate, the pile remained just as high.
The redcurrant juice in Poppy's glass
magically refilled each time she took a
sip. Through the round window, the sky
glowed a beautiful dusky pink thanks
to the work of the sunrise fairies.

When they were full, Poppy, Ninad
and Rose went to their first lesson.
Professor Whistlewind was waiting
in the map room. He was short and
round, and mostly bald apart from
some tufts of curly black hair at the
back of his head.

"Good morning to you, young

fairies," he said cheerfully.

Before Poppy had a chance to ask where they were going, he had pointed his wand at the map and muttered a command Poppy didn't hear. The air shimmered again, but this time, a flurry of snow surrounded them like they were inside a snowstorm.

Poppy brushed snow out of her eyes and looked around.

"This must be Snowflake Mountain," she gasped as a sudden gust of icy cold air whipped around them. She'd never seen snow before; it was so white and crisp and beautiful.

"You can see my house from here!"
Rose said excitedly. "Although I
normally wear something a bit warmer
when I'm here." She shivered.

Professor Whistlewind flicked his
wand and a pile of fluffy white cloaks
appeared. "Swan feathers," he said.
"Excellent for keeping you warm and
dry."

Poppy and Rose eagerly pulled on
their cloaks and Poppy immediately
felt warm and snug. The class gathered
around a patch of white snowdrops.

"This spell protects the flowers from
frost," Professor Whistlewind told them.

A spark flew at the snowdrops and they glowed for a moment, but then faded.

Professor Whistlewind frowned at his wand.

"Did the spell work?" Ninad asked.

He shook his head then shrugged. "Yes, but no magic seed. Very odd indeed. Never mind, let's make snowflakes instead."

The fairies practised making delicate snowflakes with their wands. Poppy laughed as hers spun and danced in the wind. Then, too soon, the bluebell sounded somewhere in the distance.

"Ah," said Professor Whistlewind. "Time for your next lesson." He pulled a map out of his pocket and tapped it with his wand. "OAKWINGS ACADEMY," he boomed. In an instant, they were back at Oakwings.

Poppy beamed as she saw their next teacher waiting for them in the map room.

"Aunt Li— I mean, Ms Mayblossom!" she cried, greeting her aunt.

"Where are we going this time?" Rose asked, fluttering over the map.

"Nowhere." Aunt Lily grinned. She led them down to a large greenhouse behind Oakwings Academy. It had a few tall flowers reaching high up to the glass.

"Normally," she said sadly, "the greenhouse is full of magic seeds. But since Lady Nightshade's curse, these plants might be the last ones we have to make fairy dust."

Rose gasped and Ninad held up his hand nervously.

"So it's true?" he asked. "Lady Nightshade really has cursed the forest?"

"I don't know for sure," Aunt Lily replied. "But none of us have been able to collect any seeds since she appeared."

The fairies whispered amongst themselves, then Ms Mayblossom gave the cheery smile that Poppy knew and loved.

"Enough of that," she said. "Let me show you how to make the flowers grow."

"Listen to my fairy song,
Flowers grow tall and strong . . ."

As she repeated the song, the class joined in. As they sang, the seeds and plants around them quivered and swayed back and forth. They even seemed to like Ninad's off-key singing.

As the bluebell went and the others flew out, Poppy hung back to talk to Aunt Lily. "Will there really be no more fairy magic without the seeds?" Poppy asked.

"When a fairy does something helpful, such as helping an animal in need, a magic seed appears. Those seeds are brought here where we sing and help them to grow," Aunt Lily said,

showing Poppy a bright blue flower
that had just opened. Inside was a
sparkly golden powder.

"This is fairy dust," she told Poppy.
"It is inside our wands, and helps us
to use our magic – apart from fungus
fairies, who don't use wands. Without
magic seeds, the whole fairy kingdom
is in trouble." She sighed sadly. "But the
teachers are looking after it, Poppy. All
you need to think about is your lessons.
And shouldn't you be in one now?"

"Whoops, yes, I've got my first lesson
with Ms Webcap," Poppy said, giving
her aunt a quick hug.

"Third classroom from the left, right down in the tree roots," Aunt Lily called as Poppy rushed out of the greenhouse.

"You're late!" Ms Webcap said when Poppy arrived. Her classroom was dark and smelled mossy and damp.

"Sorry, Ms Webcap," Poppy replied.

Ms Webcap smiled sweetly. "No matter," she said. "Take a seat."

Poppy sat between Ninad and Rose. There was a huge pile of mushrooms on the desk in front of them.

"What are we supposed to do?" Poppy whispered.

Rose grimaced. "We have to count

the mushrooms," she said.

Poppy crinkled her nose. "For a spell?"

Ninad shrugged.

Ms Webcap seemed nice enough, but there was something about her that Poppy didn't quite trust. As she counted bright red mushrooms, Poppy thought about what Aunt Lily had said about the magic seeds.

"We should be using our magic to break Lady Nightshade's curse," she whispered, "Not counting mushrooms!"

"Fungus magic is just as important as the magic in your wand," Ms Webcap said. "Just because it is not bright and flashy like sunshine, or icy cold like snow, doesn't mean that it is any less *powerful*. Fungus is neither animal or plant, it is a unique living thing and that is what makes it truly special."

Poppy glanced at Ms Webcap's hat as she spoke. For a moment she thought it moved, and she remembered the black beady eyes she'd seen. She stared at it suspiciously, but it didn't move again.

"Do you need something, Poppy?"

Ms Webcap said, catching her staring.

"Um, yes, how can fungus help?" Poppy asked.

For a second Ms Webcap looked angry, but then she smiled. "Why don't you and your friends go and do a detention outside, collecting mushrooms in the forest," she said, her voice high and tinkly. "Maybe then you'll appreciate fungus a little bit more."

Celeste smirked at the front of the classroom.

"At least we're not counting mushrooms any more," Poppy sighed once they were outside, looking around

in the long grass in front of Oakwings Academy. "I'm sorry you had to come with me."

Rose nudged Poppy's shoulder. "I'd rather be out here with you."

"I'm going to be in so much trouble when my parents hear about this," Ninad groaned.

Although it was supposed to be a punishment, Poppy found that being in the forest with her best friends was actually quite fun. At least, until the sky began to darken.

Ninad pointed to a long, dark shadow moving through the trees.

"What's that?" he squeaked.

Poppy peered through the darkness. The shadow was heading towards the school. Fast.

"It could be Lady Nightshade," she cried, flying towards it.

Rose raced after her.

"If it is Lady Nightshade, shouldn't we be flying in the *opposite* direction?" Ninad cried.

But as Poppy neared the old oak tree she saw that it wasn't Lady Nightshade, but Ottalie the little otter.

"Help!" cried Ottalie. "Please fairies, I need help!"

Chapter Six

The otter banged at the door of Oakwings Academy as hard as she could. The huge oak door opened and the shadow of Ms Webcap loomed over Ottalie.

"I . . . need . . . help!" Ottalie panted, trying to catch her breath.

"What happened?" Poppy asked as they reached her.

Ottalie's paws trembled. "The river has dried up, and my brother Ollie is missing."

Poppy's eyes grew wide. How could the river have dried up so suddenly? It had been full when they were there yesterday.

She flew over to Ottalie, Rose and Ninad right behind her. "We'll help!" she said eagerly.

Rose and Ninad nodded. "What can we do?"

"You three will do *nothing*," Ms Webcap said, sternly. "This is not a job for young fairies who barely know how to use their wands."

She looked down at Ottalie. "It's
nearly the students' bedtime," she said.
"We will send help in the morning."

Ottalie looked terrified. "But . . . I
need help now!"

Ms Webcap glared at Ottalie. "I said goodnight."

She ushered Poppy, Rose and Ninad inside and closed the heavy door with a loud bang, then flew off.

"Ms Webcap, wait!" Poppy shouted, chasing after her. "*We* can help Ottalie."

"We should at least try," Rose agreed.

Ms Webcap paused. "I'm sure the otter will find his way home. Now get to bed, all of you."

Poppy opened her mouth to protest but Ms Webcap held up a hand. "Not another word, Miss Merrymoss."

"Poor little Ollie," Ninad sniffed. "He

must be so scared."

Poppy clenched her fists as they flew to their rooms. "I know we haven't learned a lot of magic yet, but we could still help search for Ollie."

Ninad shook his head. "You heard Ms Webcap."

Poppy and Rose said goodnight to Ninad and flew to their room. Small fairy lights strung around the window and bunk beds gave out a warm glow. Celeste snored quietly in her bed.

But Poppy knew she wouldn't be able to sleep a wink while Ollie was in trouble.

"We have to do something, Rose," she cried.

Rose hugged Poppy. "We'll go out and help as soon as the sun rises."

"But what if it's too late by then?" Poppy whispered. She looked out of the window and then looked back at Rose determinedly. "I'm going to help Ottalie now."

Rose sighed. "Well, I'm not going to let you have all the fun," she said, squeezing Poppy's hand.

Poppy smiled at her friend gratefully. They sneaked out of their room as quietly as they could.

"Look,
there's Spot,"
Rose said as
they crept along
the hallway.

Poppy knelt
down. "Can you wake
up Ninad?" she asked the ladybird.
"Tell him to meet us in the map room."

Spot waved one of his legs then flew
off.

A few minutes later Ninad met them
in the map room. His scruffy brown
hair was ruffled and his glasses sat
lopsided on his face.

Poppy took a deep breath. "We're going to help Ottalie."

Ninad frowned. "We're going to be in so much trouble if Ms Webcap finds out."

"You don't have to come, Ninad," Rose said kindly.

Ninad shook his head. "I want to help the otters."

Poppy tapped her wand on the map just as the teachers had done. "I hope this works."

She closed her eyes and imagined she was back at the river with the gently flowing water and the breeze through

the trees. "RAINBOW RIVER," she commanded. She held her breath, worried her magic might not work, but to her surprise the air began to shimmer.

"It's working!" Rose cried.

Poppy gasped as they appeared beside the river. There was barely a trickle of water along the drying riverbed.

The forest looked strange in the darkness. Shadows crept across the ground. Strange noises called out from the trees above. The only light they had to guide them came from the moon. They called out for Ottalie.

Suddenly there was a loud cracking noise. Ninad jumped. "Lady Nightshade!" he yelled.

"Wait," Poppy said, listening carefully. Then she smiled as she heard a small squeak. "It's Ottalie!"

Ottalie smiled gratefully at them all. "Oh, thank you for coming, fairies!" she gasped. "We've all been looking, but we haven't found him." She pointed her paw at where a group of all kinds of animals were searching the dried-up river.

"Let's see what's happened to the river," Poppy said. "That might lead us to your brother."

They flew along the riverbed, with Ottalie racing after them, until they discovered the problem.

A gigantic pile of rubbish – plastic bottles, bags, wrappers – was all twisted

and caught up amongst leaves and
twigs. It made a wide dam across the
river, holding back the water on the
other side.

"Why can't the humans take their
rubbish home with them?"
Rose said sadly.

A tiny squeak came from
the pile and the fairies
froze. Ottalie climbed up
the rubbish mountain.

"It's Ollie!" she
called out. "He's
trapped!"

Chapter Seven

Poppy, Rose and Ninad flew over to help Ottalie. The fairies started pulling at the plastic and wrappers, removing them bit by bit. Poppy wished that they'd learnt some magic that could help. Some of the pieces of rubbish were almost as big as they were!

The more they cleared, the more water trickled through the gaps they'd

made, until a gentle rush of water
flowed.

"Ollie is still stuck!" Ottalie called
out. She was crouched next to her little
brother, holding his paw.

"Let me help," said Ninad. He flew
over to Ottalie and the two of them
tried gently tugging at Ollie's paws.
But before they could pull him free,
there was a loud crack and crash as
a thundering wave of water broke
through the remaining rubbish.

"Ollie!" Ottalie cried.

Ninad tried to hang on to Ollie's
paw, but the water knocked them both

into the river, soaking Ninad's wings.

Poppy and Rose flew to try and grab the tiny otter, but the water was flowing too fast and the baby otter was swept away.

Ninad flapped out of the water, coughing and spluttering.

"Use your fairy magic!" Ottalie cried.

"We only know one spell!" Rose said, her eyes wide.

"Then we'll have to use that one!" Poppy said.

Rose and Ninad nodded and the three fairies focused on the river.

"Ninad, you're the best at the raindrop spell out of all of us. Focus on Ollie and bringing him to the riverbank," Poppy said.

Ninad's face twisted in concentration. Poppy joined him. Time slowed again, until she could see each individual water drop in the river. She moved one, then another and another. With Ninad's help, the water started to flow in a different direction, moving Ollie to the river's edge. But it still wasn't quite enough.

"Rose!" Poppy called. "We need your help too; we're stronger together."

Rose gave Poppy a determined nod and held out her wand. Although she sent the water spraying everywhere, it still helped.

"Concentrate on the tip of your wand," Ninad told her.

Rose did, and gradually her wand sprayed less and less. "I'm doing it!" she squeaked.

Bit by bit, the tiny otter moved closer to the shore until he was close enough for Ottalie to jump in and grab him.

"Thank you!" she cried out. She hugged Ollie tight and sobbed as the baby otter coughed and spluttered.

Poppy breathed out in relief.

The tiny otter looked up at the fairies. "Thank you!" he squeaked.

Poppy, Rose and Ninad grinned and hugged each other. The rubbish was cleared and the river was flowing as normal. Poppy felt a thrill of pride as she realised that they'd done it – they'd really helped! Just then she noticed something shimmering in the shallow water.

"What's that?" She reached in and pulled it out.

It was the size and shape of a seed. Blue, with speckled white spots just like

the stars in the
night sky.

"Could it be
. . . a magic
seed?" Poppy
wondered.

"We should take
it to Ms Mayblossom,"
Rose said. "If it *is* a magical seed,
maybe Lady Nightshade's curse hasn't
worked after all!"

"I wish we had a map like the
teachers do," Ninad grumbled. "Then
we could just magic ourselves back
rather than flying all the way."

"I know a fun way to get you back," Ottalie said. "A starlight river ride!"

They followed Ottalie to the river, and she pulled a large piece of loose bark from a nearby tree then placed it at the water's edge.

"Hop on!" Ottalie called as she jumped onto another piece of bark a little way ahead.

Poppy, Rose and Ninad carefully climbed onto the floating wooden raft. They pushed off, then it zoomed down the river at lightning speed. The forest whizzed past as they went. More otters joined them on their journey, dancing

in the water beside them.

Poppy and Rose whooped and laughed as they went. Ninad looked slightly green but as soon as he saw the other otters, his face split into a wide grin.

The rafts finally came to a rest at the riverbank and the fairies hopped onto dry land.

"Oakwings Academy is through those trees," Ottalie told them, pointing her paw.

"Thank you, Ottalie," Ninad said, giving her a hug.

Ottalie smiled back at them. "Thank

you for saving Ollie and our river," she said. Then, with a wave, she dived beneath the water and swam away.

They turned towards school when a loud voice boomed behind them.

"WHAT do you think you are doing?"

Poppy turned slowly to see Ms Webcap, her hands on her hips and her face as red as a raspberry.

"We had to do something," Poppy started. "Ottalie needed our help and the river . . ."

Ms Webcap noticed the seed in Poppy's arms.

"What is *that*?"
she said slowly.

"We think it's
a magic seed,"
Rose said. "When
we helped the otters, it
appeared in the water."

Ms Webcap smiled sweetly. "Give it to
me, Poppy."

Poppy took a step forward, but the
way Ms Webcap was staring at the seed
made her pause. She shook her head,
holding the seed tightly in her arms.

"Give that seed to me RIGHT
NOW!" Ms Webcap yelled.

Poppy shook her head. "I think I'll give it straight to Ms Mayblossom," she said bravely.

Ms Webcap looked furious. "After all the spells I did to get rid of those magic seeds," she growled to herself. "Perhaps the curse doesn't affect the younger fairies because they aren't a particular type yet. Still, who would have thought they would be powerful enough to make a magic seed appear . . ." She looked up suddenly as though she'd forgotten they were there.

"We were just trying to help Ollie the otter," Ninad said.

Poppy stayed quiet, watching Ms Webcap carefully. Did she say that it was *her* spells that got rid of the magic seeds?

As though she'd heard her thoughts, Ms Webcap smirked at Poppy. All at once her leafy top grew, stretching into a long cape of dead leaves. A mask appeared over her eyes and the black hat upon her head moved. It wiggled eight spindly legs as it glared at the fairies.

"It's a spider!" Rose whimpered.

Poppy's eyes widened. She hadn't imagined Ms Webcap's hat moving and the beady black eyes after all!

Ms Webcap let out a wicked cackle that made Poppy's skin crawl.

"It's Ms Webcap," Poppy stuttered, "she's Lady Nightshade!"

Chapter Eight

Ms Webcap threw out her hands and laughed. Large spiderwebs flew from them, one after the other. Poppy, Rose and Ninad dodged left and right, trying to avoid the sticky webs. But there were so many and Ms Webcap was fast.

Then Poppy had an idea.

"Rose!" she called, ducking as

another web whizzed past. "Do the water spell."

Rose looked confused. "But I still can't do it properly."

Poppy grinned. "I know!" she said.

Rose's eyes lit up as she realised what Poppy was asking her to do.

"Ninad, we need to find water," Poppy yelled.

They weaved in and out of the trees, searching for raindrops, or any small pool of water. Finally, Poppy saw a puddle ahead. It was muddy but it would have to do.

"There!" Poppy said. "Go on, Rose.

Give it your best shot!"

Rose pointed her wand at the puddle and sprayed the water in Ms Webcap's direction. Just as she had done with Celeste, except this time she did it on purpose.

Ms Webcap shrieked as the muddy water hit her in the face. Poppy and Ninad helped Rose until Ms Webcap was a dripping muddy mess. Water dribbled into her eyes and the spider growled as it shook its wet legs. While she was distracted, Poppy, Ninad and Rose dodged past her, flying as fast as they could.

"You will never prove who I really am," Ms Webcap yelled after them.

Poppy, Rose and Ninad didn't stop until the massive old oak tree came into view.

The front door was open and they barreled right into Madame Brightglow, Aunt Lily and Mr Pitterpour, sending them to the ground in a pile of wings and arms and legs.

"I told you they had sneaked out,"

Celeste said smugly, coming into view behind the teachers.

But Poppy didn't care that they were in trouble. All she cared about was Lady Nightshade and the seed.

"We went to help Ottalie," Poppy started.

"The river had dried up because of the human's rubbish," added Rose.

"Poor Ollie got caught up in it," Ninad continued.

"And Ms Webcap is Lady Nightshade," they blurted out at the same time.

Madame Brightglow glanced at

Aunt Lily and Mr Pitterpour, looking confused. But before she could speak, a cold voice spoke out behind them.

"Whatever do you mean?" Ms Webcap flew down the stairs in her normal clothes. She had beaten them back to school and was somehow completely dry and clean.

"They seem to think you are Lady Nightshade," Aunt Lily said, with a small laugh.

Ms Webcap frowned. "Oh dear, young fairy children and their silly stories. Is this because I sent you out of my classroom earlier?"

"Poppy!" Aunt Lily cried, sounding disappointed.

Mr Pitterpour cleared his throat. "I'll go and check the river."

"We are in so much trouble," Ninad whispered as the teachers whispered

amongst themselves.

Madame Brightglow turned to the young fairies. "I know it has been a worrying time for you all," she said. "But Lady Nightshade does not exist. Ms Webcap is a good teacher and you owe her an apology."

Ms Webcap smiled sweetly at the fairies, but Poppy could see the evil glittering behind her eyes.

"But she *is*—" Poppy started. But she knew the adult fairies would never believe her.

"Sorry, Ms Webcap," she mumbled, and Rose and Ninad did the same.

Mr Pitterpour burst through the front door with a wide grin on his face.

"It is true," he said. "Not about Ms Webcap being Lady Nightshade of course," he chuckled. "The animals told me what these young fairies have done. The river was so clogged up with human rubbish that it dried out. If they hadn't cleared it, the river could have flooded and destroyed many homes. We should be thanking them!"

"But they ignored my orders, sneaked out of bed and accused me of being a villain!" Ms Webcap spluttered.

"Wait!" Madame Brightglow

interrupted as she noticed the seed in Poppy's arms. "What do you have there, Poppy?"

Poppy had almost forgotten about the seed.

"I think it's a magic seed," she said, handing it to Aunt Lily. "After we helped the otters and cleared the river, it appeared in the water."

Aunt Lily examined the blue seed and her

eyes lit up. "It *is* a magic seed!" she said. "It shouldn't be possible."

Madame Brightglow smiled warmly at the fairies. "Congratulations," she said. "Not only is this your first magic seed, but it is proof that there is no curse."

"Come and help me plant your seed," Aunt Lily said to the young fairies.

"That's not fair!" Celeste complained.

"Back to bed, Celeste," Madame Brightglow ordered.

They flew to the greenhouse, where Aunt Lily found an empty pot. Rose and Ninad filled it with soil as Poppy tried to talk to Aunt Lily.

"But she *is* Lady Nightshade, Aunt Lily," Poppy insisted.

Aunt Lily sighed. "It's not like you to lie, Poppy," she said. "I believe you really think she's Lady Nightshade. I'll keep an eye on her, OK? But you three need to stop breaking the rules, or you might be expelled next time."

Ninad gulped. "There won't be a next time," he said.

Rose nodded, although Poppy noticed her fingers were crossed.

"Come on," Aunt Lily said. "I've got a special treat for you."

She led them up into the highest branches of the tree, to a small room with no roof.

"The stargazing room!" Poppy said, gazing up at the dark blue sky. The bright stars twinkled above and seemed to wink at her.

They settled down onto piles of cosy cushions. Aunt Lily waved her wand and three steaming mugs of hot chocolate appeared on a small table. "Have fun!" Aunt Lily said as she fluttered back downstairs.

Poppy picked up her drink. It was warm and delicious and she felt

instantly better after drinking it.

"I'm so glad Ollie is OK," Ninad said, sipping his drink.

"Me too," said Rose. "I can't believe that I actually did the raindrop spell!"

Poppy laughed. "You were amazing Rose," she said. "You too, Ninad. I couldn't have done it without you both."

"I still can't believe that Ms Webcap is Lady Nightshade," Ninad said under his breath.

"I'm not sure the grown-ups will ever believe us," Poppy said quietly. "Even Aunt Lily thinks we're making it up."

"Ms Mayblossom is right though," Rose said. "We need to be more careful around Ms Webcap now."

Poppy nodded. "And if they won't believe us, we'll just have to stop her ourselves," she said. The three friends nodded as they sipped their hot chocolates and stared up at the beautiful stars high above. They wouldn't let Lady Nightshade ruin fairy forest, no matter what!

The End

It's time for the Blossom Fair and all the fairies are so excited! But Poppy and her friends can't enjoy the picnic or their bunny babysitting ... because mean Lady Nightshade is determined to cause trouble again!

Find out what happens in:
Baby Bunny Magic

Poppy and her friends are off on a school trip to the Snowflake Mountains! There are snowball fights, a cute arctic fox and everyone is excited about the Winter Ball. But Lady Nightshade wants the powerful magic of the snow fairies for herself ...

Find out what happens in:

The Snowflake Charm